*Dedicated with love to my
amazing Mum – there would be
no Tall Man without you*
TNC

*For my family –
the short and the tall*
DN

by
Tom Niland Champion
Kilmeny Niland

pictures by
Deborah Niland

ALLEN&UNWIN

THE TALL MAN

and the twelve babies

In a big,
big city,

in a tiny,
tiny apartment

lived a tall,
tall man ...

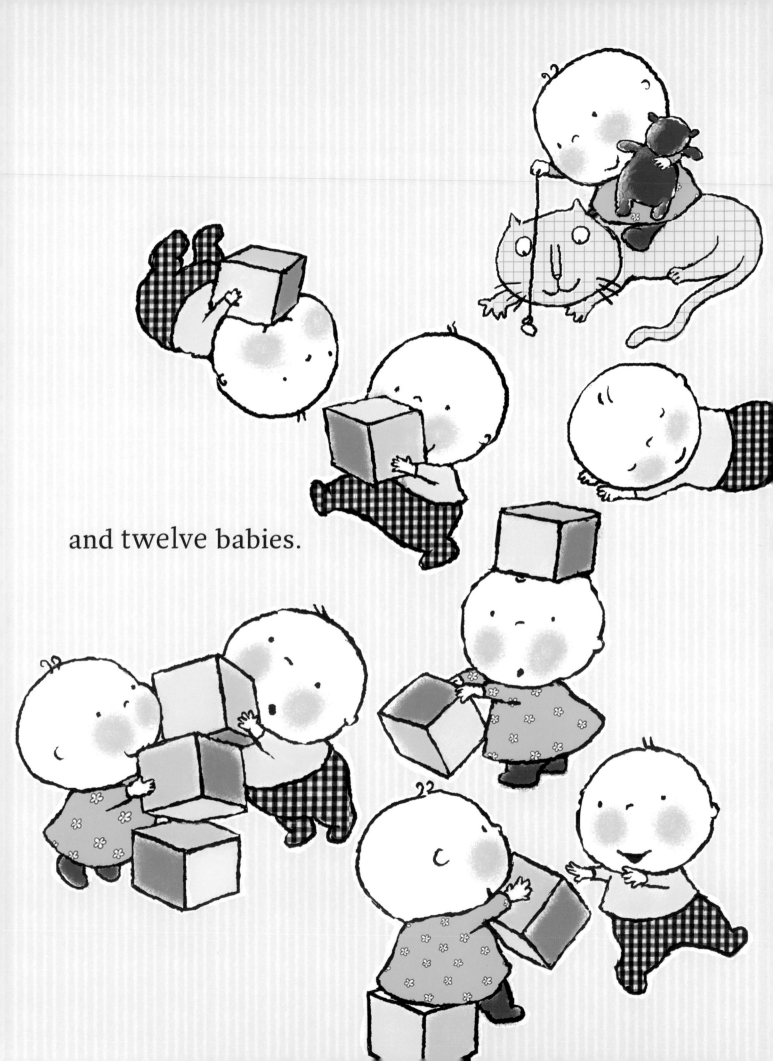

and twelve babies.

Every morning,
the **tall man** counted his twelve babies.
1-2-3-4-5-6-7-8-9-10-11-12 babies …
and then he fed them **mashed banana**.

All the boys were called Alistair.
All the girls were called Charlene.

When the twelve babies were happy,
they all laughed at the same time.

When the twelve babies were angry,
they all yelled at the same time.
Sometimes the tall man yelled too.

One grey afternoon,
the twelve babies were very, very lively.

Charlene was bouncing Alistair off the couch.
Alistair was jingling the keys.
Charlene was biting Alistair.
Alistair was chasing the cat.

'Charlene, Alistair!
Stop messing around!'
said the **tall** man.

But no one was listening.

The tall man
scooped up the cat
and the Charlenes
and stepped outside.

'Quick! Alistair,'

the tall man called through the cat flap.

'Bring me the keys!'

But the Alistairs were busy.

'Oh, pussywillow,'

said the tall man.

He stretched his long, long arms
through the narrow cat flap,
but right in the middle
he got stuck.

The babies were delighted!
The Charlenes surfed
on his long, long legs.

The Alistairs played
with his curly, curly hair.

'Alistair!
Charlene!

Pull me out!'

the tall man shouted.

So the Charlenes pulled one way

and the Alistairs pulled the other way.
But the tall man didn't budge.

'STOP!

You'll pull me in two!'

'Alistair pull and Charlene push
on the count of three,'
yelled the tall man.

'1-2-3...'

WHOOOOOOOOSH...

The **tall** man popped through the flap,
followed by six tumbling Charlenes
and one flying cat.

The **tall** man was so happy to be
back with his twelve babies.
He picked them up and kissed them all,
one by one.

Every Charlene.
Every Alistair.

That evening,
the **tall** man fed them mashed potato
and counted his twelve babies.

1-2-3-4-5-6-7-8-9-10-11 babies ...

Uh oh ...
where's Alistair?

First published in 2010

Allen & Unwin
83 Alexander Street
Crows Nest NSW 2065
Australia
Phone (612) 8425 0100
Fax (612) 9906 2218
Email info@allenandunwin.com
Web www.allenandunwin.com

Cataloguing-in-Publication details are available
from the National Library of Australia
www.trove.nla.gov.au

ISBN 978 1 74237 115 3

Design by Bruno Herfst and Deborah Niland
Artwork by Deborah Niland
Set in 20pt Fresco

This book was printed in September 2011 at Everbest
Printing Co Ltd in 334 Huanshi Road South,
Nansha, Guangdong, China.

10 9 8 7 6 5 4 3